MARVEL
SUPER HERO SQUAD

LOVE IS IN THE AIR!

WRITER: Todd Dezago
ARTISTS: Leonel Castellani & Marcelo DiChiara
COLORS: Sotocolor
LETTERS: Dave Sharpe

ASSISTANT EDITOR: Michael Horwitz
EDITOR: Nathan Cosby

Spotlight

Visit us at www.abdopublishing.com

Reinforced library bound edition published in 2011 by Spotlight, a division of the ABDO Group, 8000 West 78th Street, Edina, Minnesota 55439. Spotlight produces high-quality reinforced library bound editions for schools and libraries. Published by agreement with Marvel Characters, Inc.

Printed in the United States of America, North Mankato, Minnesota.
102010
012011
♻ This book contains at least 10% recycled materials.

Library of Congress Cataloging-in-Publication Data

Dezago, Todd.
  Love is in the air! / Todd Dezago, writer ; Leonel Castellani & Marcelo DiChiara, artists ; Sotocolor, colors ; Dave Sharpe, letters. -- Reinforced library bound ed.
     p. cm. -- (Super hero squad)
"Marvel."
 ISBN 978-1-59961-860-9
 1. Graphic novels. [1. Graphic novels. 2. Superheroes--Fiction.] I. Castellani, Leonel, ill. II. Dichiara, Marcelo, ill. III. Title.
 PZ7.7.D508Lo 2011
 741.5'973--dc22
                                        2010027324

All Spotlight books have reinforced library bindings and are manufactured in the United States of America.

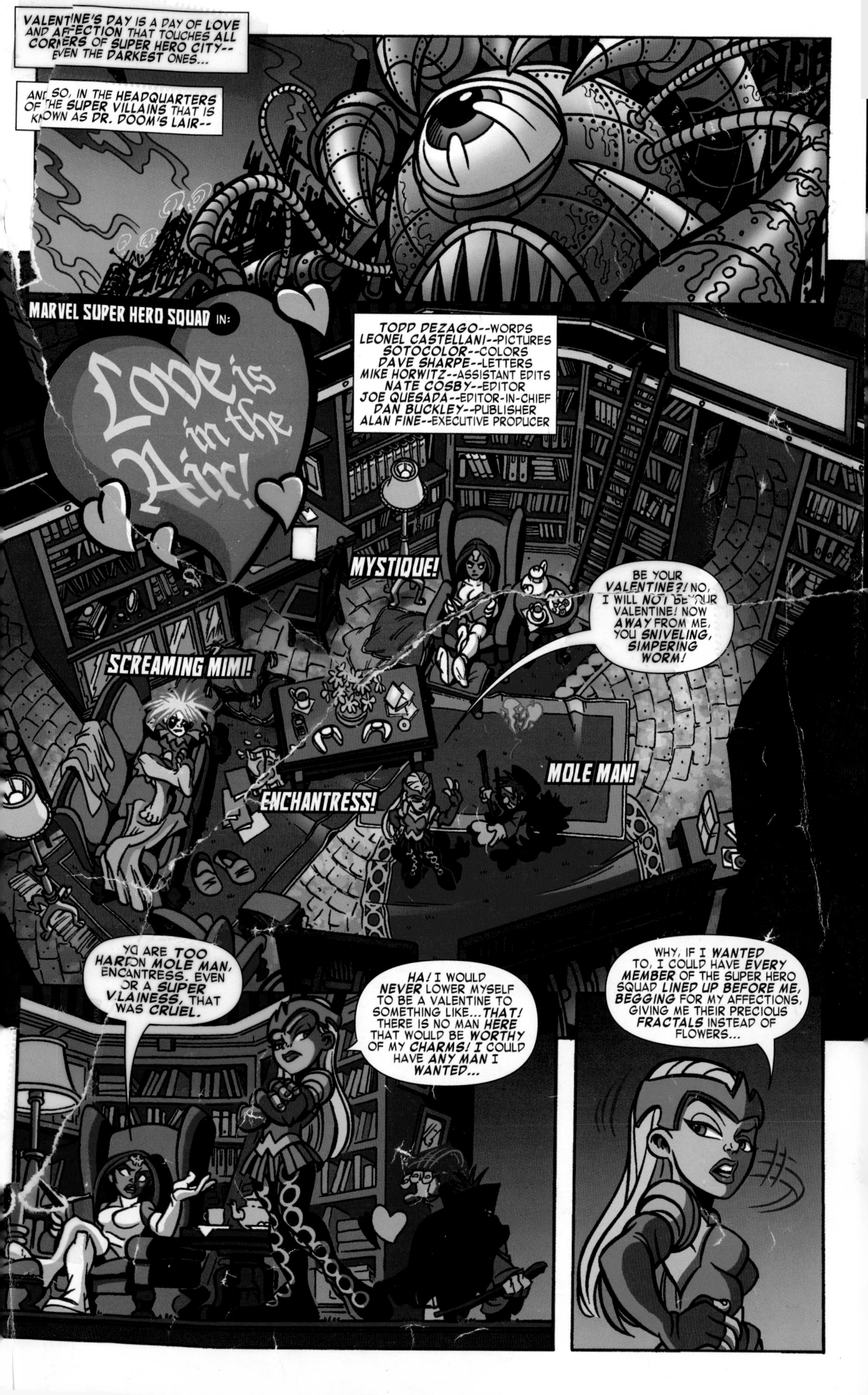
VALENTINE'S DAY IS A DAY OF LOVE AND AFFECTION THAT TOUCHES ALL CORNERS OF SUPER HERO CITY-- EVEN THE DARKEST ONES...
AND SO, IN THE HEADQUARTERS OF THE SUPER VILLAINS THAT IS KNOWN AS DR. DOOM'S LAIR--
MARVEL SUPER HERO SQUAD IN:
Love is in the Air!
TODD DEZAGO--WORDS
LEONEL CASTELLANI--PICTURES
SOTOCOLOR--COLORS
DAVE SHARPE--LETTERS
MIKE HORWITZ--ASSISTANT EDITS
NATE COSBY--EDITOR
JOE QUESADA--EDITOR-IN-CHIEF
DAN BUCKLEY--PUBLISHER
ALAN FINE--EXECUTIVE PRODUCER
MYSTIQUE!
SCREAMING MIMI!
ENCHANTRESS!
MOLE MAN!
BE YOUR VALENTINE?! NO, I WILL NOT BE YOUR VALENTINE! NOW AWAY FROM ME, YOU SNIVELING, SIMPERING WORM!
YOU ARE TOO HARD ON MOLE MAN, ENCHANTRESS. EVEN FOR A SUPER VILLAINESS, THAT WAS CRUEL.
HA! I WOULD NEVER LOWER MYSELF TO BE A VALENTINE TO SOMETHING LIKE...THAT! THERE IS NO MAN HERE THAT WOULD BE WORTHY OF MY CHARMS! I COULD HAVE ANY MAN I WANTED...
WHY, IF I WANTED TO, I COULD HAVE EVERY MEMBER OF THE SUPER HERO SQUAD LINED UP BEFORE ME, BEGGING FOR MY AFFECTIONS, GIVING ME THEIR PRECIOUS FRACTALS INSTEAD OF FLOWERS...

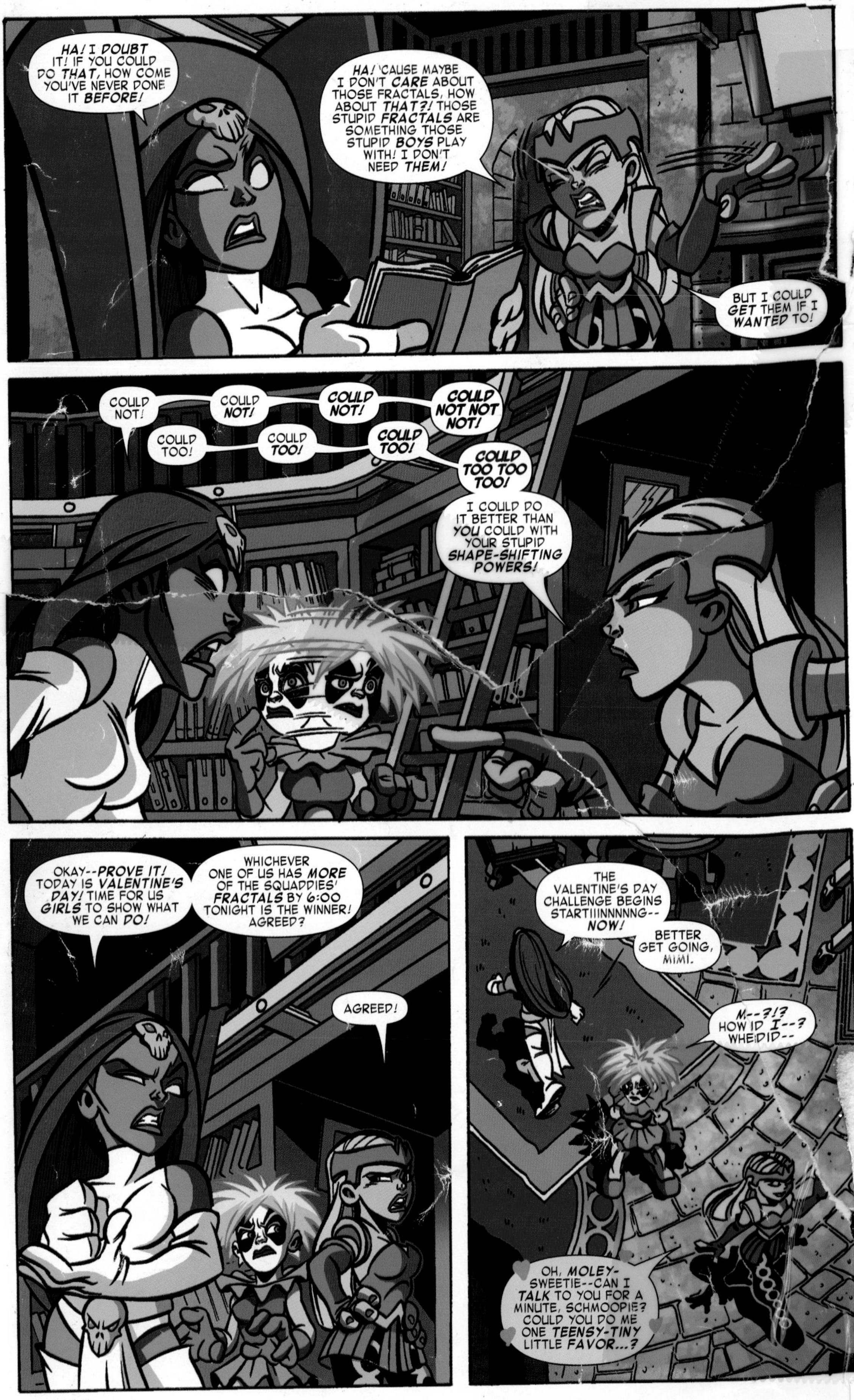
HA! I DOUBT IT! IF YOU COULD DO THAT, HOW COME YOU'VE NEVER DONE IT BEFORE!
HA! 'CAUSE MAYBE I DON'T CARE ABOUT THOSE FRACTALS, HOW ABOUT THAT?! THOSE STUPID FRACTALS ARE SOMETHING THOSE STUPID BOYS PLAY WITH! I DON'T NEED THEM!
BUT I COULD GET THEM IF I WANTED TO!
COULD NOT!
COULD TOO!
COULD NOT!
COULD TOO!
COULD NOT!
COULD TOO!
COULD NOT NOT NOT!
COULD TOO TOO TOO!
I COULD DO IT BETTER THAN YOU COULD WITH YOUR STUPID SHAPE-SHIFTING POWERS!
OKAY--PROVE IT! TODAY IS VALENTINE'S DAY! TIME FOR US GIRLS TO SHOW WHAT WE CAN DO!
WHICHEVER ONE OF US HAS MORE OF THE SQUADDIES' FRACTALS BY 6:00 TONIGHT IS THE WINNER! AGREED?
AGREED!
THE VALENTINE'S DAY CHALLENGE BEGINS STARTIIIINNNNNG--NOW!
BETTER GET GOING, MIMI.
M--?!? HOW ID I--? WHE:DID--
OH, MOLEY-SWEETIE--CAN I TALK TO YOU FOR A MINUTE, SCHMOOPIE? COULD YOU DO ME ONE TEENSY-TINY LITTLE FAVOR...?

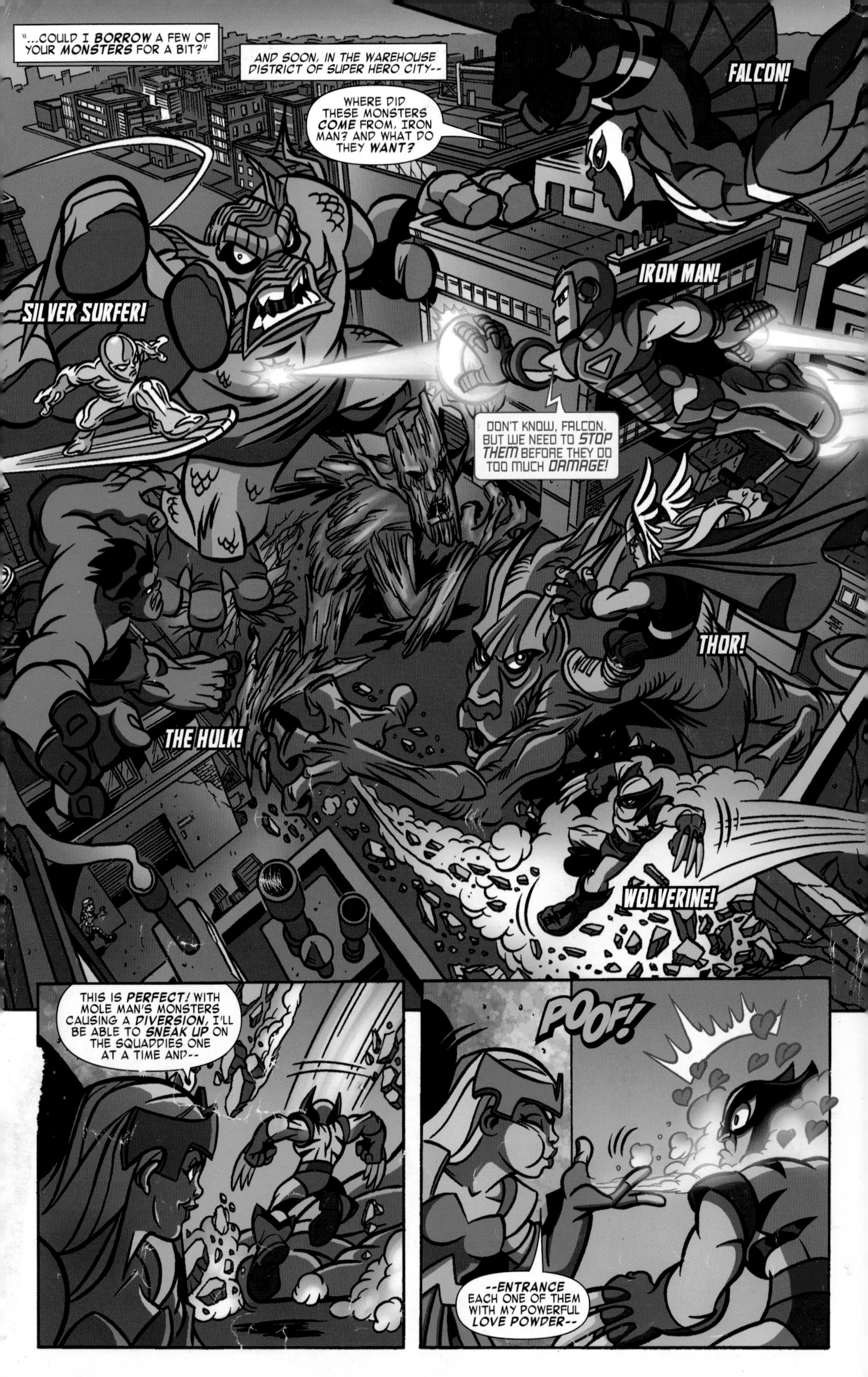
"...COULD I BORROW A FEW OF YOUR MONSTERS FOR A BIT?"
AND SOON, IN THE WAREHOUSE DISTRICT OF SUPER HERO CITY--
WHERE DID THESE MONSTERS COME FROM, IRON MAN? AND WHAT DO THEY WANT?
FALCON!
IRON MAN!
SILVER SURFER!
DON'T KNOW, FALCON. BUT WE NEED TO STOP THEM BEFORE THEY DO TOO MUCH DAMAGE!
THOR!
THE HULK!
WOLVERINE!
THIS IS PERFECT! WITH MOLE MAN'S MONSTERS CAUSING A DIVERSION, I'LL BE ABLE TO SNEAK UP ON THE SQUADDIES ONE AT A TIME AND--
POOF!
--ENTRANCE EACH ONE OF THEM WITH MY POWERFUL LOVE POWDER--

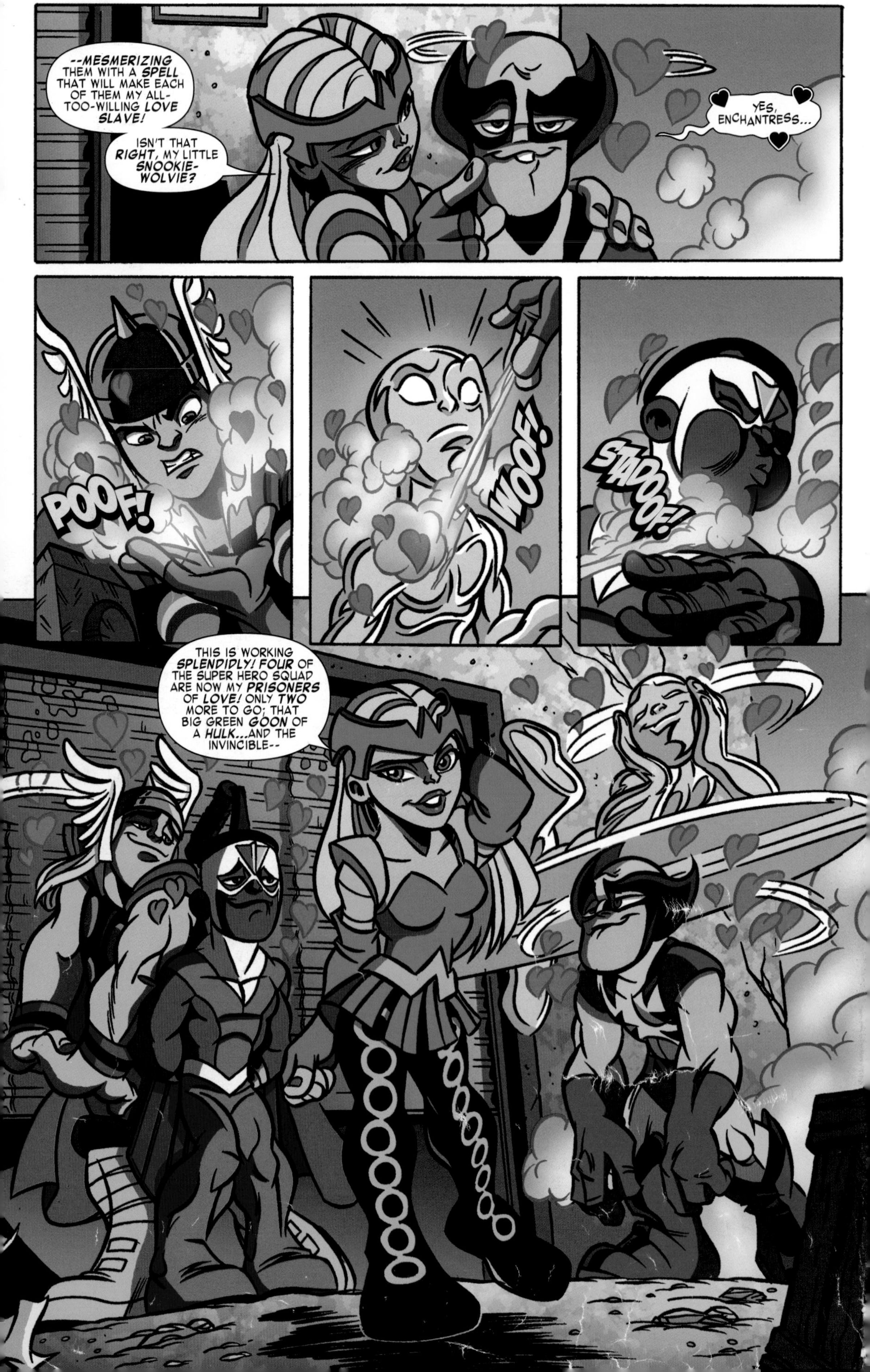

--MESMERIZING THEM WITH A SPELL THAT WILL MAKE EACH OF THEM MY ALL-TOO-WILLING LOVE SLAVE!
ISN'T THAT RIGHT, MY LITTLE SNOOKIE-WOLVIE?
YES, ENCHANTRESS...
POOF!
WOOF!
STADOOOF!
THIS IS WORKING SPLENDIDLY! FOUR OF THE SUPER HERO SQUAD ARE NOW MY PRISONERS OF LOVE! ONLY TWO MORE TO GO; THAT BIG GREEN GOON OF A HULK...AND THE INVINCIBLE--

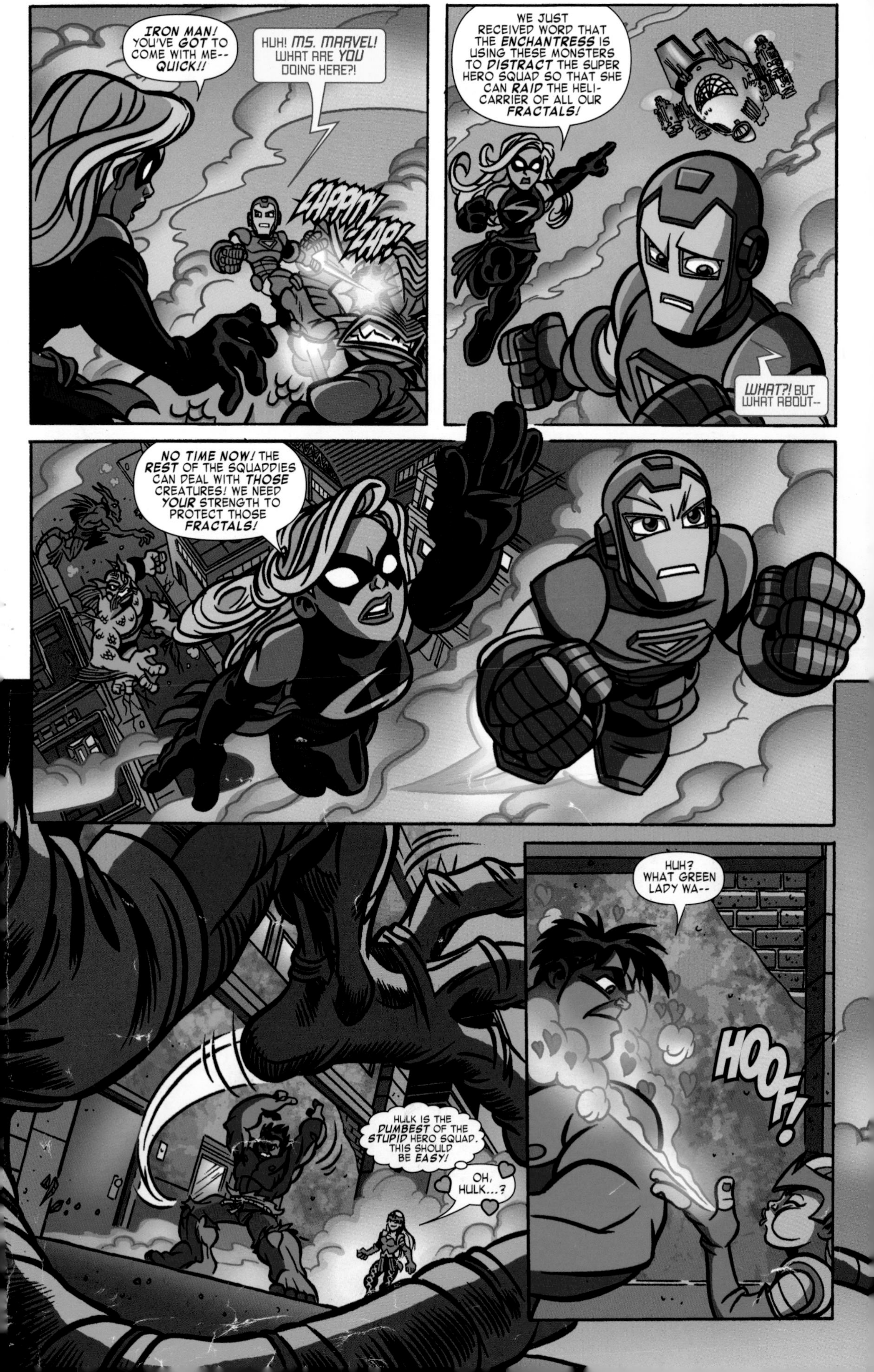
IRON MAN! YOU'VE GOT TO COME WITH ME-- QUICK!!
HUH! MS. MARVEL! WHAT ARE YOU DOING HERE?!
ZAPPITY ZAP!
WE JUST RECEIVED WORD THAT THE ENCHANTRESS IS USING THESE MONSTERS TO DISTRACT THE SUPER HERO SQUAD SO THAT SHE CAN RAID THE HELI-CARRIER OF ALL OUR FRACTALS!
WHAT?! BUT WHAT ABOUT--
NO TIME NOW! THE REST OF THE SQUADDIES CAN DEAL WITH THOSE CREATURES! WE NEED YOUR STRENGTH TO PROTECT THOSE FRACTALS!
HULK IS THE DUMBEST OF THE STUPID HERO SQUAD. THIS SHOULD BE EASY!
OH, HULK...?
HUH? WHAT GREEN LADY WA--
HOOF!

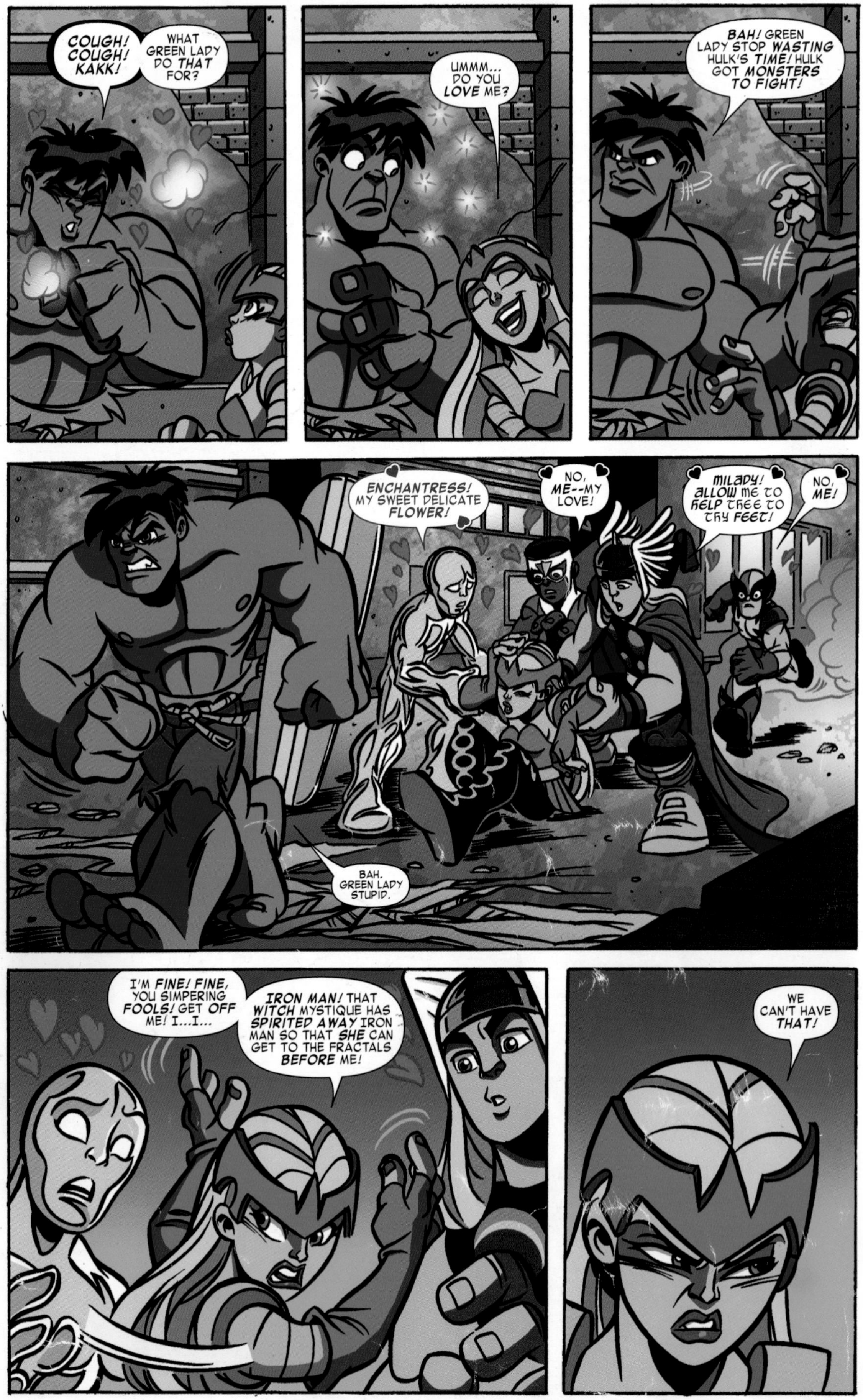
COUGH! COUGH! KAKK!
WHAT GREEN LADY DO THAT FOR?
UMMM... DO YOU LOVE ME?
BAH! GREEN LADY STOP WASTING HULK'S TIME! HULK GOT MONSTERS TO FIGHT!
ENCHANTRESS! MY SWEET DELICATE FLOWER!
NO, ME--MY LOVE!
MILADY! ALLOW ME TO HELP THEE TO THY FEET!
NO, ME!
BAH. GREEN LADY STUPID.
I'M FINE! FINE, YOU SIMPERING FOOLS! GET OFF ME! I...I...
IRON MAN! THAT WITCH MYSTIQUE HAS SPIRITED AWAY IRON MAN SO THAT SHE CAN GET TO THE FRACTALS BEFORE ME!
WE CAN'T HAVE THAT!

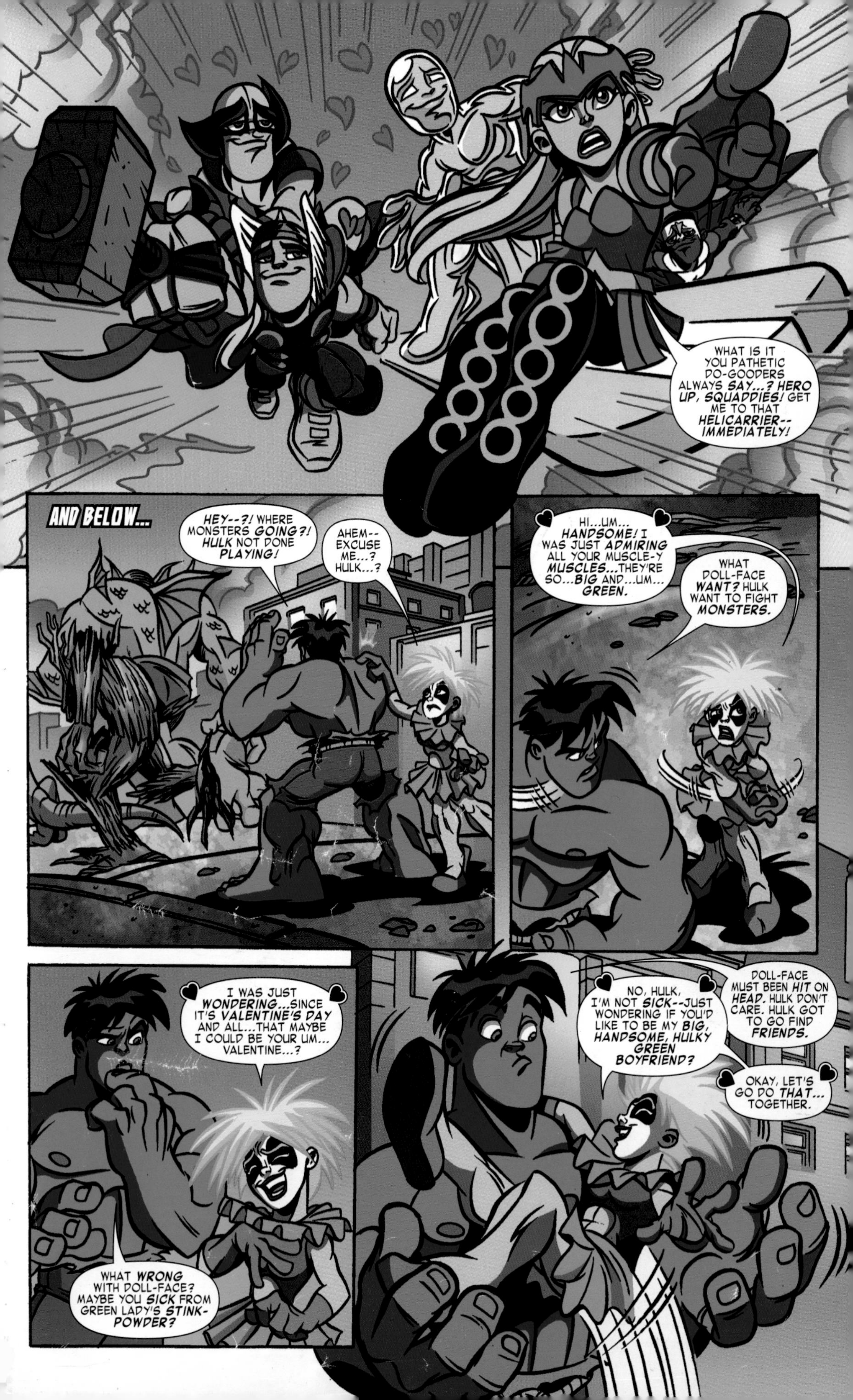
WHAT IS IT YOU PATHETIC DO-GOODERS ALWAYS SAY...? HERO UP, SQUADDIES! GET ME TO THAT HELICARRIER-- IMMEDIATELY!
AND BELOW...
HEY--?! WHERE MONSTERS GOING?! HULK NOT DONE PLAYING!
AHEM-- EXCUSE ME...? HULK...?
HI...UM... HANDSOME! I WAS JUST ADMIRING ALL YOUR MUSCLE-Y MUSCLES...THEY'RE SO...BIG AND...UM... GREEN.
WHAT DOLL-FACE WANT? HULK WANT TO FIGHT MONSTERS.
I WAS JUST WONDERING...SINCE IT'S VALENTINE'S DAY AND ALL...THAT MAYBE I COULD BE YOUR UM... VALENTINE...?
WHAT WRONG WITH DOLL-FACE? MAYBE YOU SICK FROM GREEN LADY'S STINK-POWDER?
NO, HULK, I'M NOT SICK--JUST WONDERING IF YOU'D LIKE TO BE MY BIG, HANDSOME, HULKY GREEN BOYFRIEND?
DOLL-FACE MUST BEEN HIT ON HEAD. HULK DON'T CARE. HULK GOT TO GO FIND FRIENDS.
OKAY, LET'S GO DO THAT... TOGETHER.

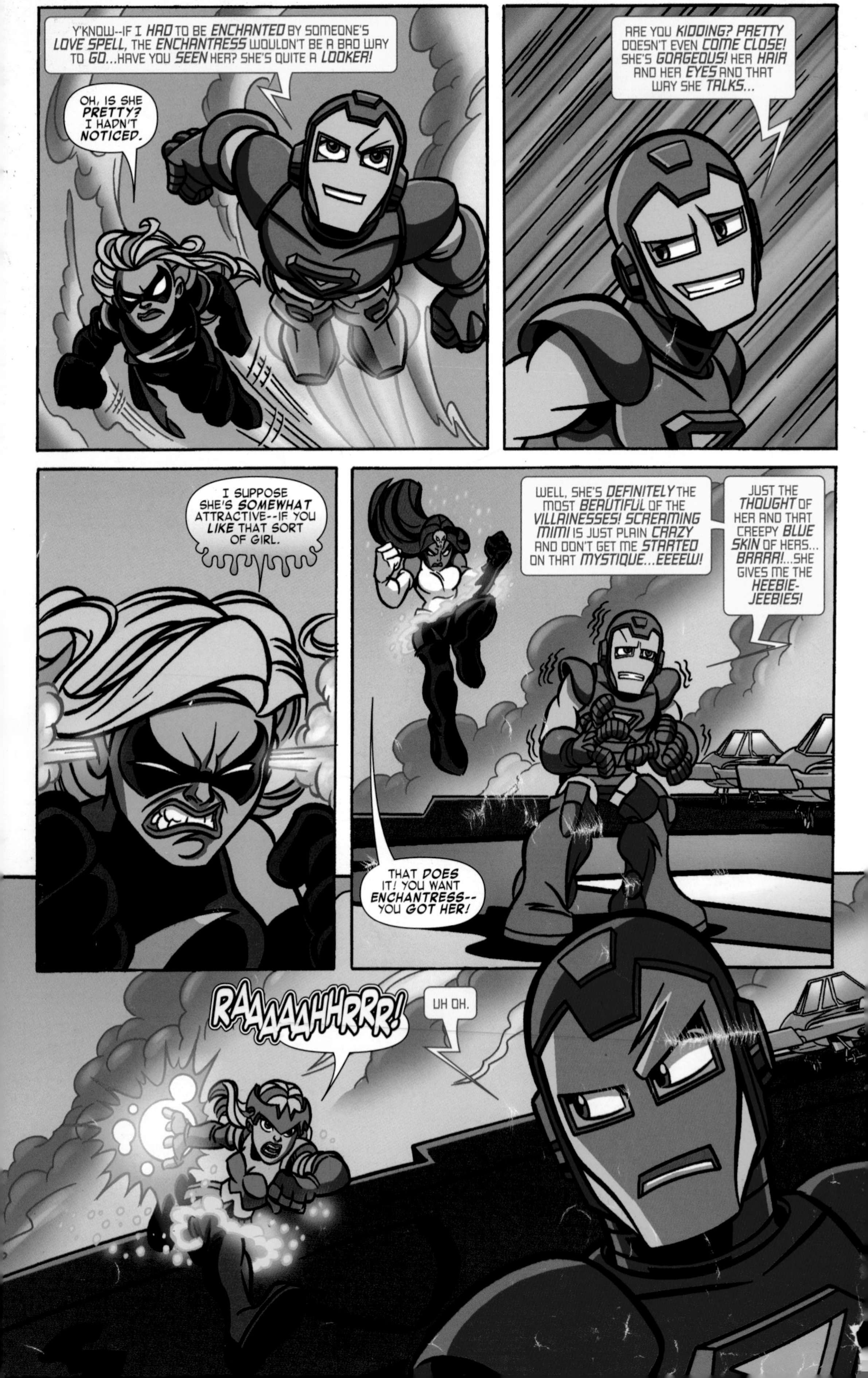
Y'KNOW--IF I HAD TO BE ENCHANTED BY SOMEONE'S LOVE SPELL, THE ENCHANTRESS WOULDN'T BE A BAD WAY TO GO...HAVE YOU SEEN HER? SHE'S QUITE A LOOKER!
OH, IS SHE PRETTY? I HADN'T NOTICED.
ARE YOU KIDDING? PRETTY DOESN'T EVEN COME CLOSE! SHE'S GORGEOUS! HER HAIR AND HER EYES AND THAT WAY SHE TALKS...
I SUPPOSE SHE'S SOMEWHAT ATTRACTIVE--IF YOU LIKE THAT SORT OF GIRL.
WELL, SHE'S DEFINITELY THE MOST BEAUTIFUL OF THE VILLAINESSES! SCREAMING MIMI IS JUST PLAIN CRAZY AND DON'T GET ME STARTED ON THAT MYSTIQUE...EEEEW!
JUST THE THOUGHT OF HER AND THAT CREEPY BLUE SKIN OF HERS... BRRRR!...SHE GIVES ME THE HEEBIE-JEEBIES!
THAT DOES IT! YOU WANT ENCHANTRESS--YOU GOT HER!
RAAAAAHHRRR!
UH OH.

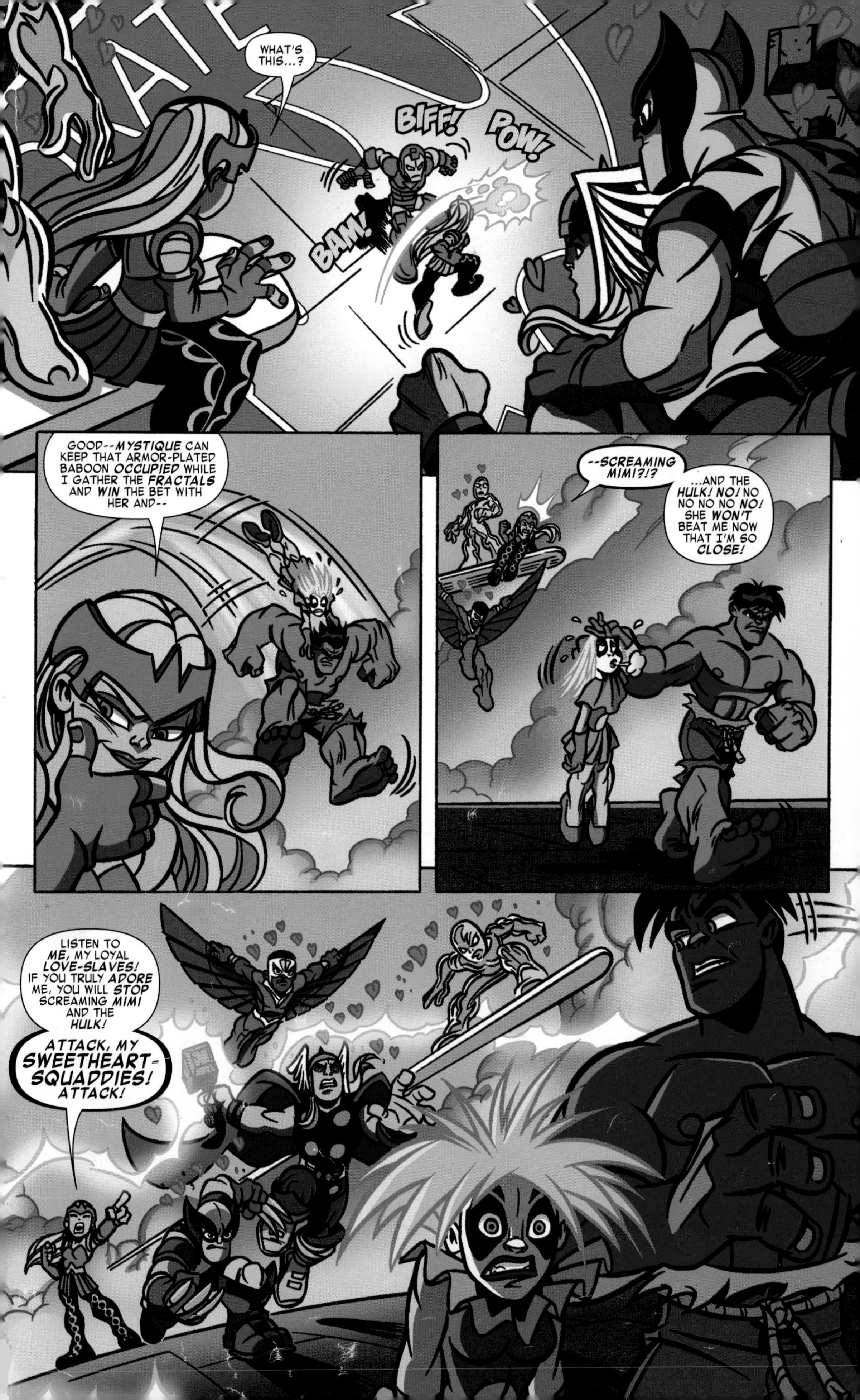
WHAT'S THIS...?
BIFF!
POW!
BAM!
GOOD--MYSTIQUE CAN KEEP THAT ARMOR-PLATED BABOON OCCUPIED WHILE I GATHER THE FRACTALS AND WIN THE BET WITH HER AND--
--SCREAMING MIMI?!?
...AND THE HULK! NO! NO NO NO NO NO! SHE WON'T BEAT ME NOW THAT I'M SO CLOSE!
LISTEN TO ME, MY LOYAL LOVE-SLAVES! IF YOU TRULY ADORE ME, YOU WILL STOP SCREAMING MIMI AND THE HULK!
ATTACK, MY SWEETHEART-SQUADDIES! ATTACK!

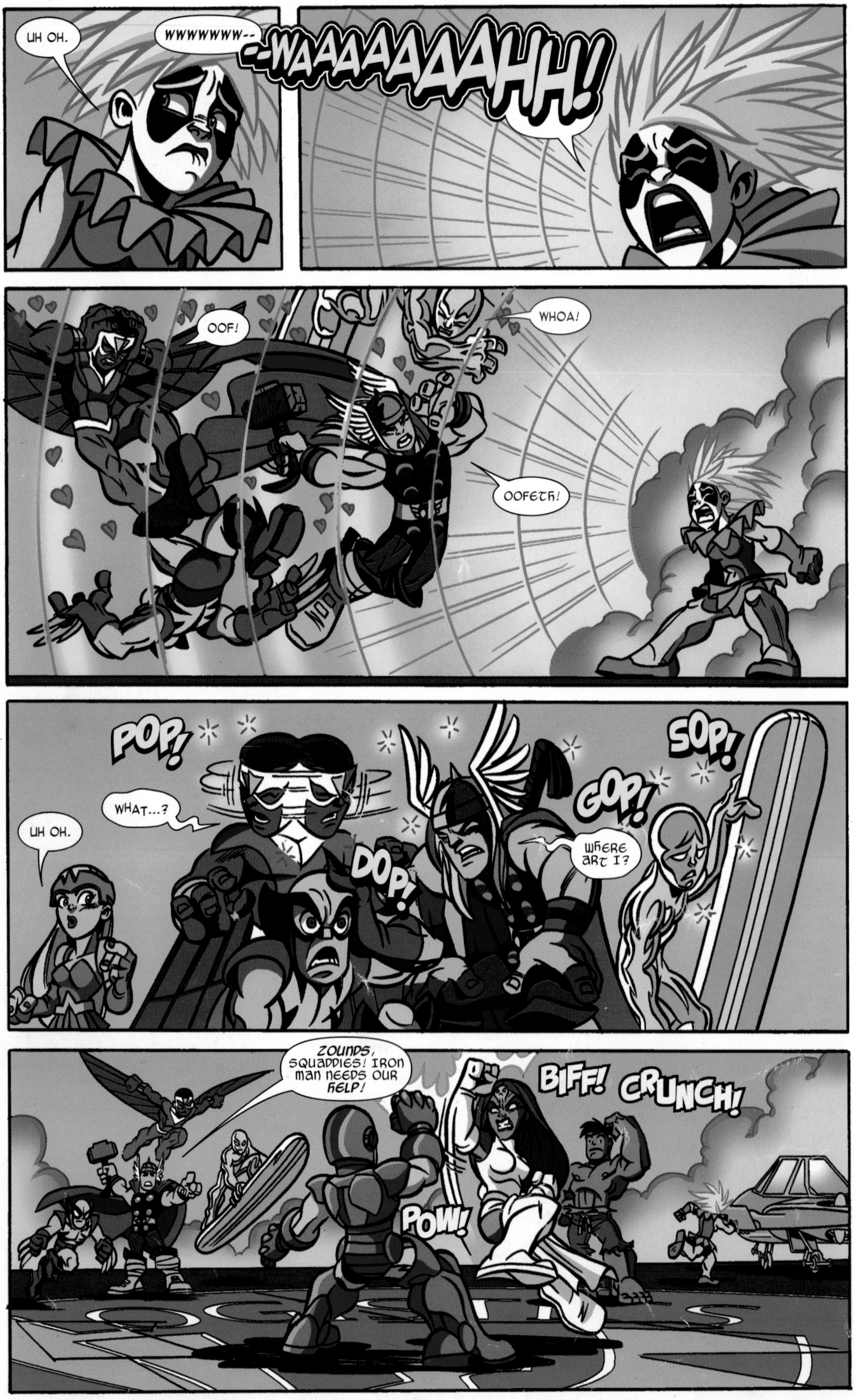
UH OH.
WWWWWWW--
--WAAAAAAAHH!
OOF!
WHOA!
OOFETH!
POP!
WHAT...?
UH OH.
DOP!
GOP!
SOP!
WHERE ART I?
ZOUNDS, SQUADDIES! IRON MAN NEEDS OUR HELP!
BIFF!
CRUNCH!
POW!

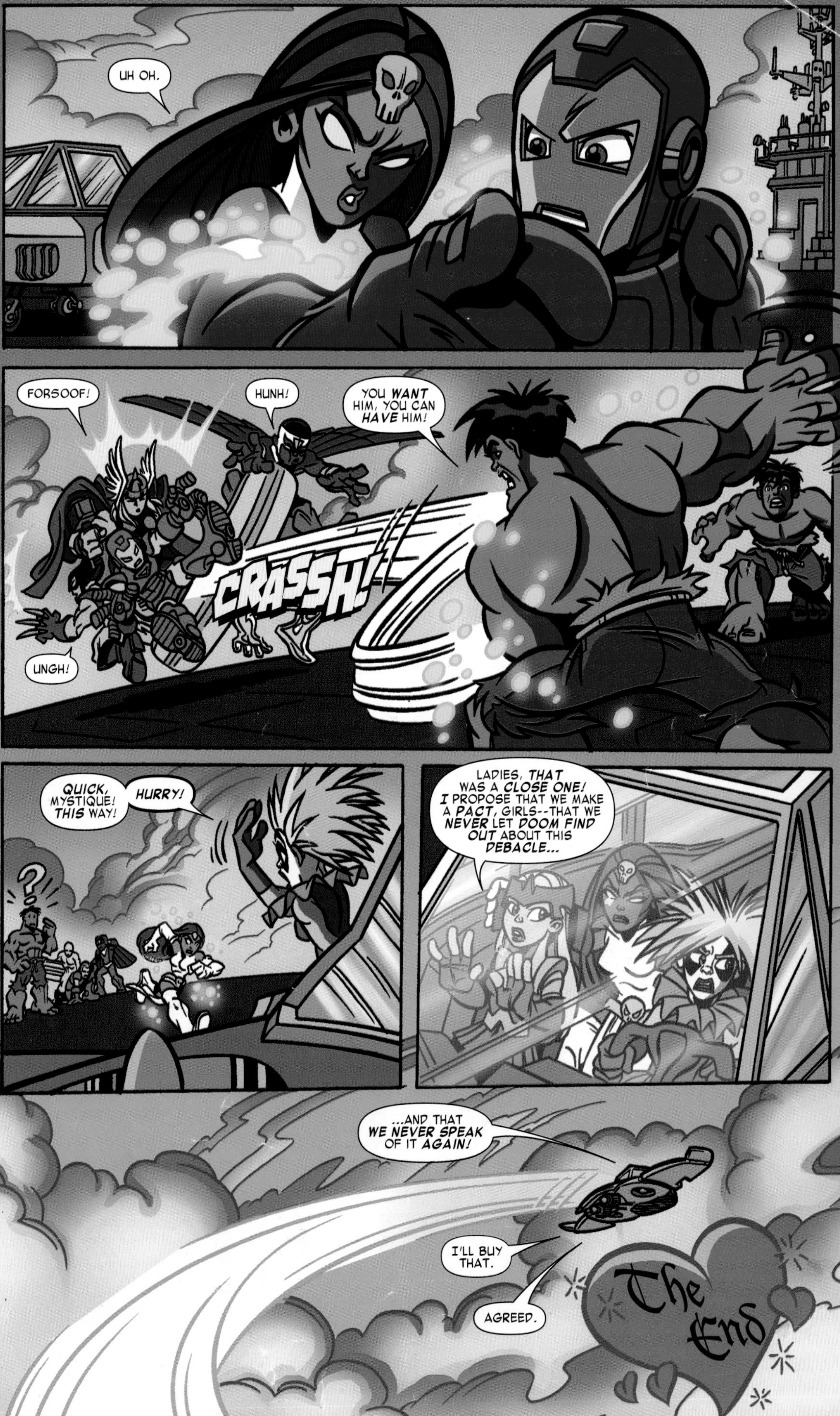
UH OH.
FORSOOF!
HUNH!
YOU WANT HIM, YOU CAN HAVE HIM!
CRASSH!
UNGH!
QUICK, MYSTIQUE! THIS WAY!
HURRY!
LADIES, THAT WAS A CLOSE ONE! I PROPOSE THAT WE MAKE A PACT, GIRLS--THAT WE NEVER LET DOOM FIND OUT ABOUT THIS DEBACLE...
...AND THAT WE NEVER SPEAK OF IT AGAIN!
I'LL BUY THAT.
AGREED.
The End

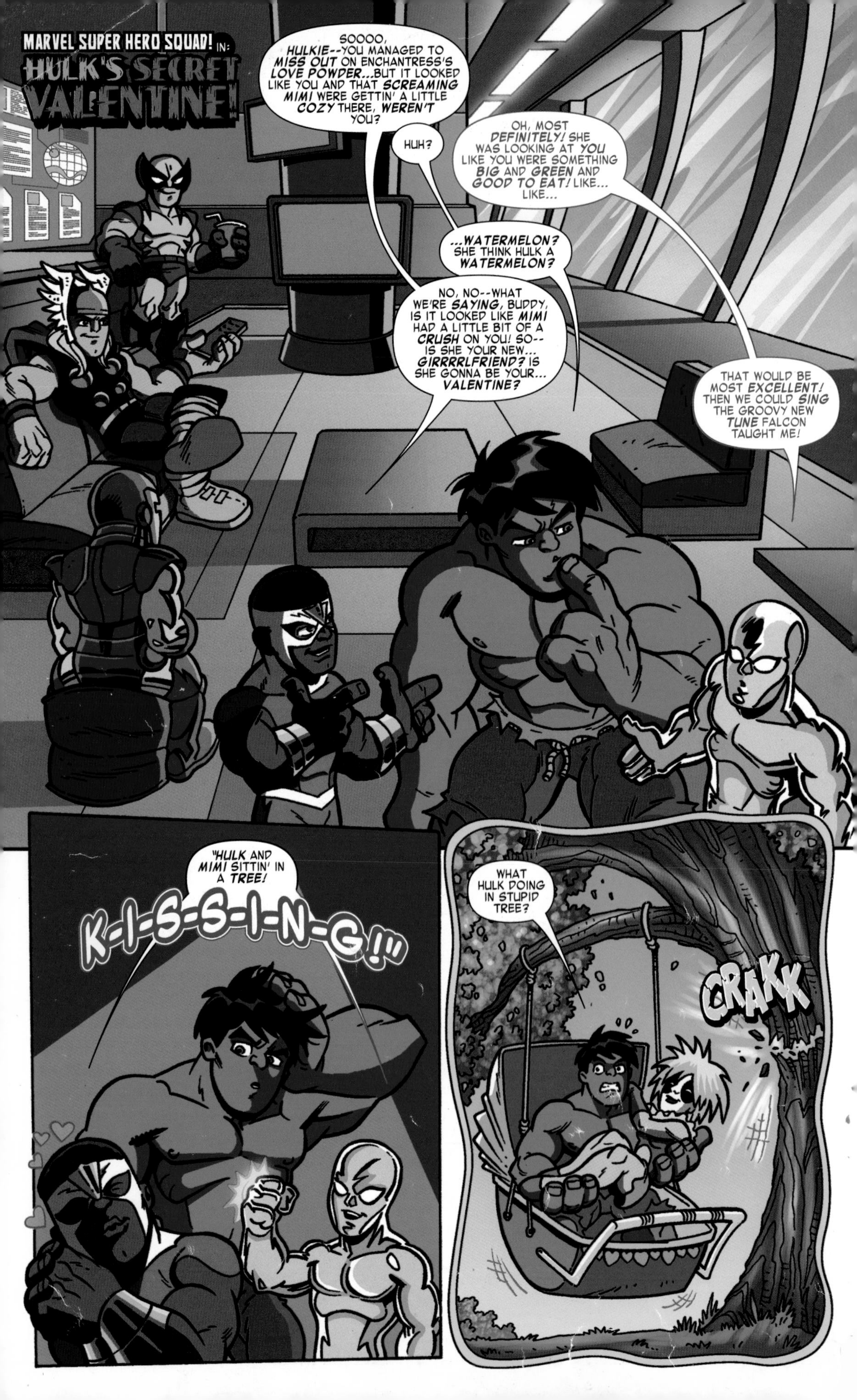
MARVEL SUPER HERO SQUAD! IN:
HULK'S SECRET VALENTINE!
SOOOO, HULKIE--YOU MANAGED TO MISS OUT ON ENCHANTRESS'S LOVE POWDER...BUT IT LOOKED LIKE YOU AND THAT SCREAMING MIMI WERE GETTIN' A LITTLE COZY THERE, WEREN'T YOU?
HUH?
OH, MOST DEFINITELY! SHE WAS LOOKING AT YOU LIKE YOU WERE SOMETHING BIG AND GREEN AND GOOD TO EAT! LIKE... LIKE...
...WATERMELON? SHE THINK HULK A WATERMELON?
NO, NO--WHAT WE'RE SAYING, BUDDY, IS IT LOOKED LIKE MIMI HAD A LITTLE BIT OF A CRUSH ON YOU! SO--IS SHE YOUR NEW... GIRRRRLFRIEND? IS SHE GONNA BE YOUR... VALENTINE?
THAT WOULD BE MOST EXCELLENT! THEN WE COULD SING THE GROOVY NEW TUNE FALCON TAUGHT ME!
"HULK AND MIMI SITTIN' IN A TREE!
K-I-S-S-I-N-G!"
WHAT HULK DOING IN STUPID TREE?
CRAKK

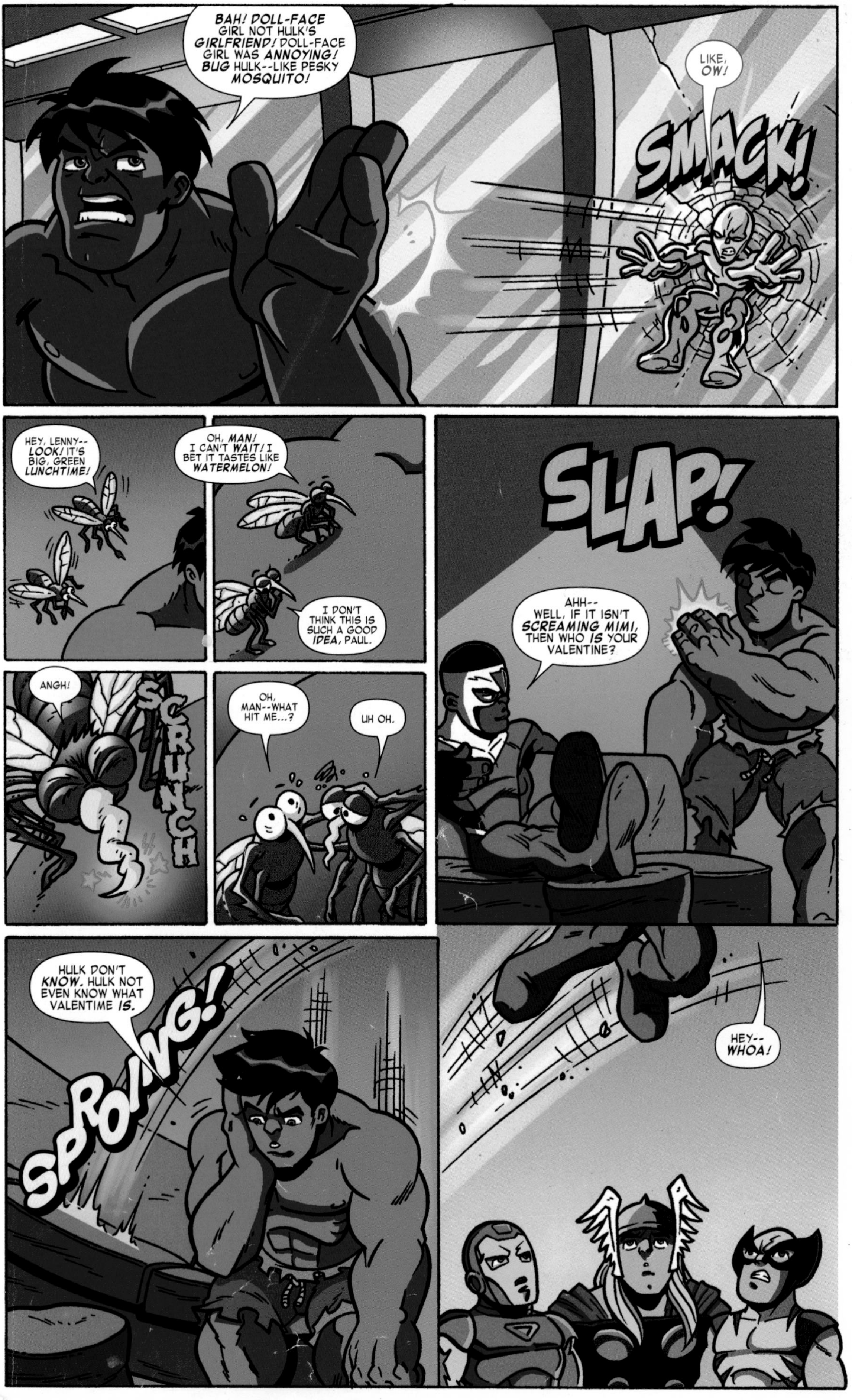
BAH! DOLL-FACE GIRL NOT HULK'S GIRLFRIEND! DOLL-FACE GIRL WAS ANNOYING! BUG HULK--LIKE PESKY MOSQUITO!
LIKE, OW!
SMACK!
HEY, LENNY--LOOK! IT'S BIG, GREEN LUNCHTIME!
OH, MAN! I CAN'T WAIT! I BET IT TASTES LIKE WATERMELON!
I DON'T THINK THIS IS SUCH A GOOD IDEA, PAUL.
SLAP!
AHH--WELL, IF IT ISN'T SCREAMING MIMI, THEN WHO IS YOUR VALENTINE?
ANGH!
SCRUNCH
OH, MAN--WHAT HIT ME...?
UH OH.
HULK DON'T KNOW. HULK NOT EVEN KNOW WHAT VALENTIME IS.
SPROING!
HEY--WHOA!

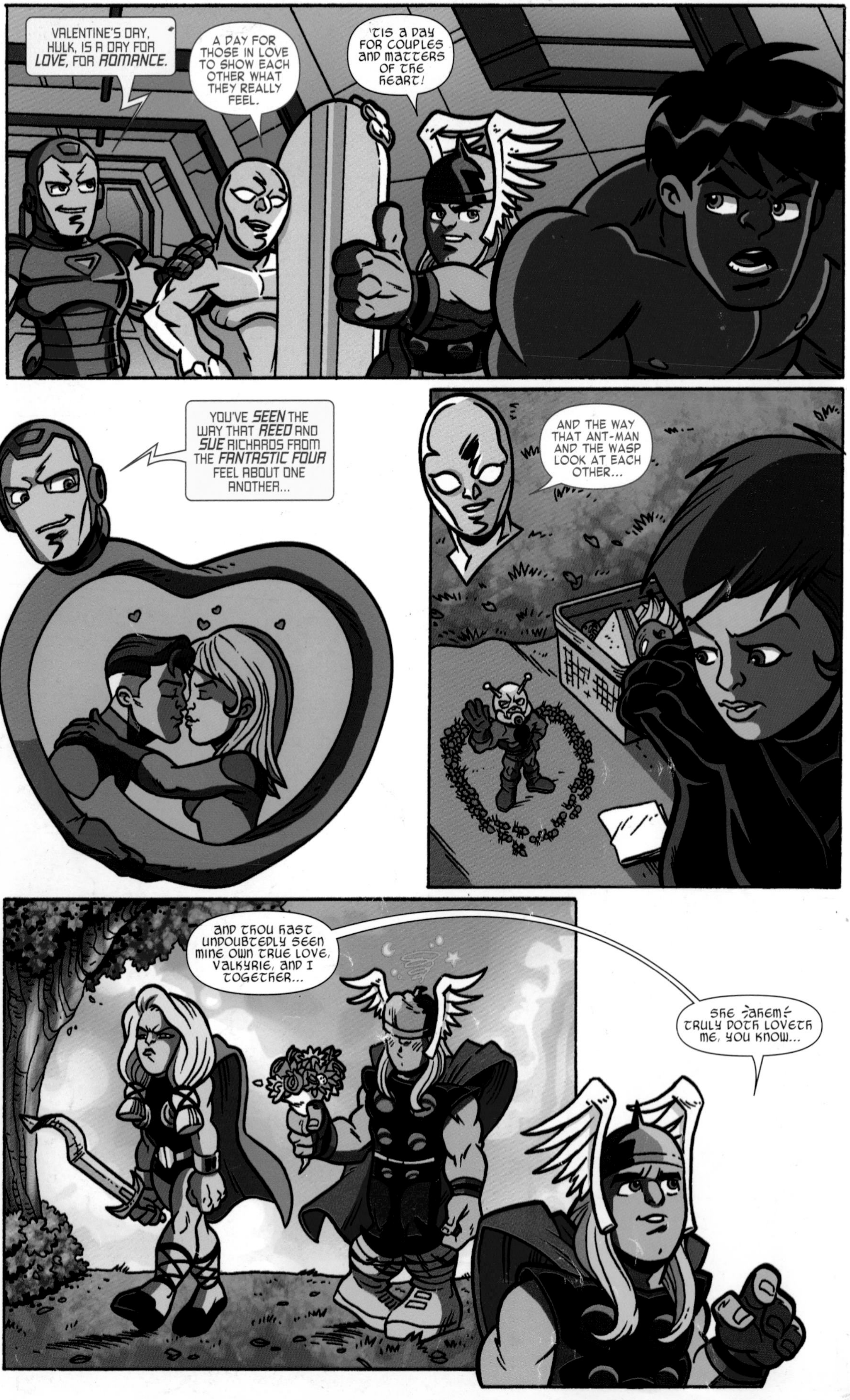

VALENTINE'S DAY, HULK, IS A DAY FOR LOVE, FOR ROMANCE.
A DAY FOR THOSE IN LOVE TO SHOW EACH OTHER WHAT THEY REALLY FEEL.
'TIS A DAY FOR COUPLES AND MATTERS OF THE HEART!
YOU'VE SEEN THE WAY THAT REED AND SUE RICHARDS FROM THE FANTASTIC FOUR FEEL ABOUT ONE ANOTHER...
AND THE WAY THAT ANT-MAN AND THE WASP LOOK AT EACH OTHER...
AND THOU HAST UNDOUBTEDLY SEEN MINE OWN TRUE LOVE, VALKYRIE, AND I TOGETHER...
SHE -AHEM- TRULY DOTH LOVETH ME, YOU KNOW...

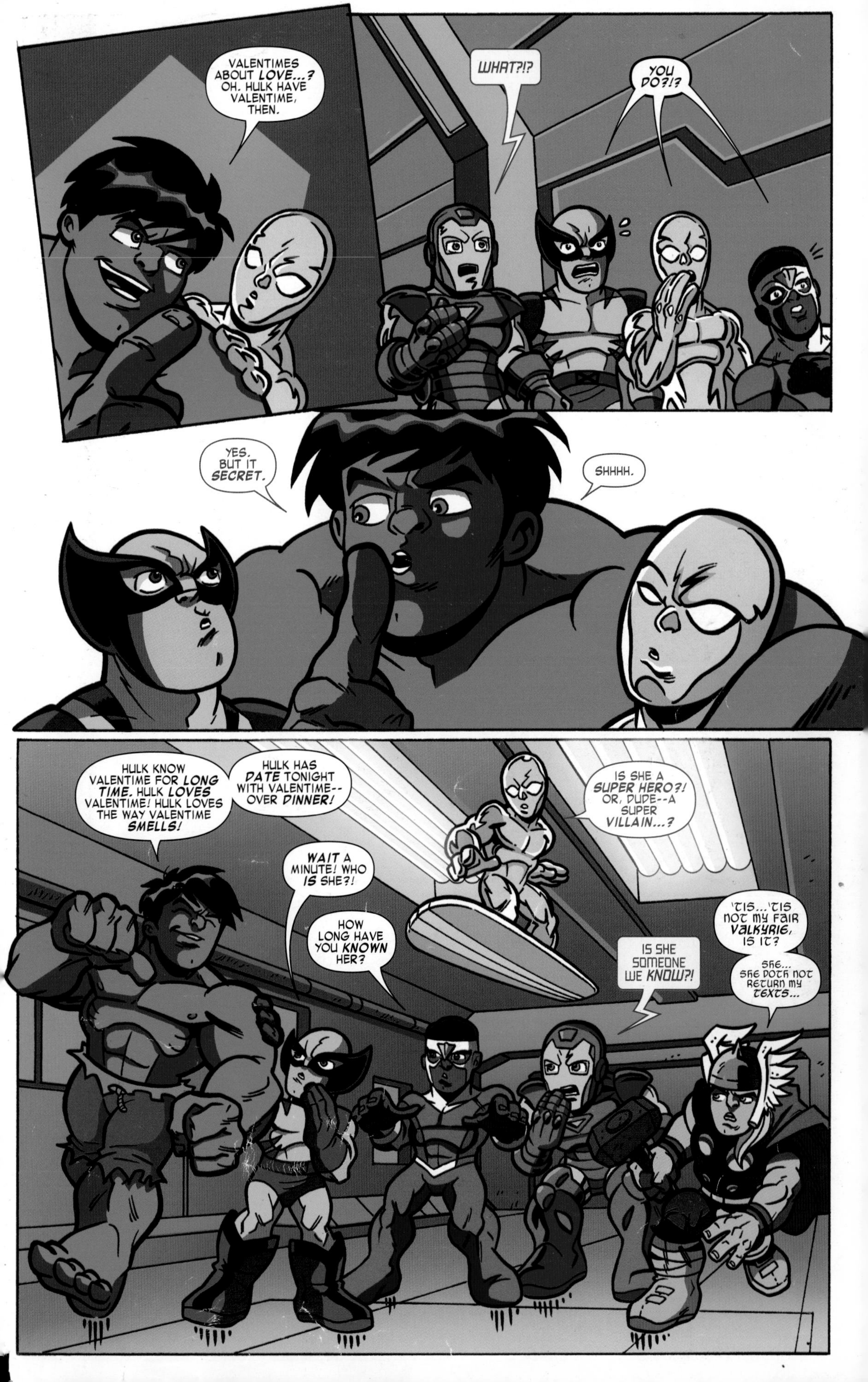
VALENTIMES ABOUT LOVE...? OH. HULK HAVE VALENTIME, THEN.
WHAT?!?
YOU DO?!?
YES. BUT IT SECRET.
SHHHH.
HULK KNOW VALENTIME FOR LONG TIME. HULK LOVES VALENTIME! HULK LOVES THE WAY VALENTIME SMELLS!
HULK HAS DATE TONIGHT WITH VALENTIME-- OVER DINNER!
IS SHE A SUPER HERO?! OR, DUDE--A SUPER VILLAIN...?
WAIT A MINUTE! WHO IS SHE?!
HOW LONG HAVE YOU KNOWN HER?
IS SHE SOMEONE WE KNOW?!
'TIS...'TIS NOT MY FAIR VALKYRIE, IS IT?
SHE... SHE DOTH NOT RETURN MY TEXTS...

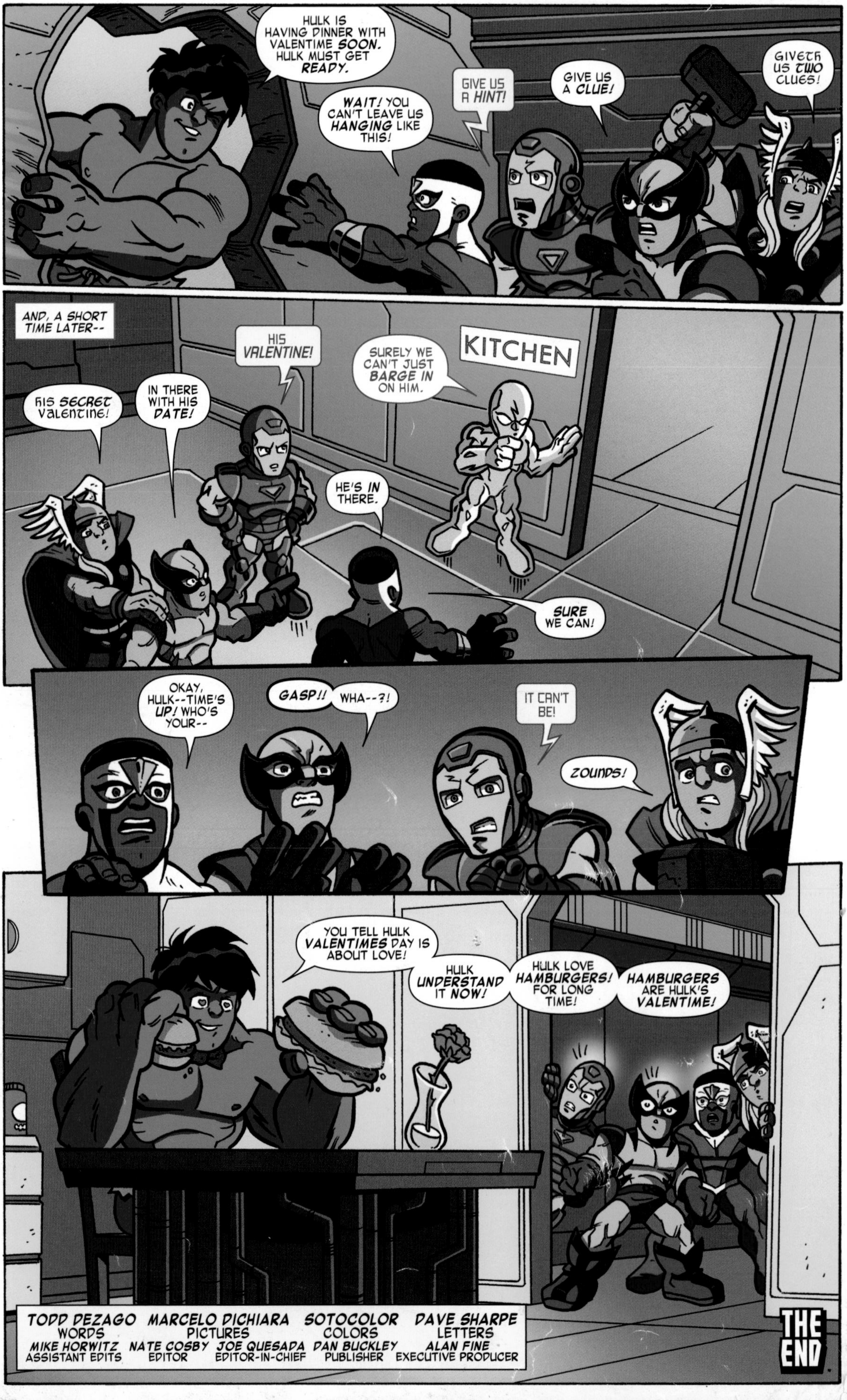
HULK IS HAVING DINNER WITH VALENTIME SOON. HULK MUST GET READY.
WAIT! YOU CAN'T LEAVE US HANGING LIKE THIS!
GIVE US A HINT!
GIVE US A CLUE!
GIVETH US TWO CLUES!
AND, A SHORT TIME LATER--
HIS SECRET VALENTINE!
IN THERE WITH HIS DATE!
HIS VALENTINE!
SURELY WE CAN'T JUST BARGE IN ON HIM.
KITCHEN
HE'S IN THERE.
SURE WE CAN!
OKAY, HULK--TIME'S UP! WHO'S YOUR--
GASP!!
WHA--?!
IT CAN'T BE!
ZOUNDS!
YOU TELL HULK VALENTIMES DAY IS ABOUT LOVE!
HULK UNDERSTAND IT NOW!
HULK LOVE HAMBURGERS! FOR LONG TIME!
HAMBURGERS ARE HULK'S VALENTIME!
TODD DEZAGO WORDS
MARCELO DICHIARA PICTURES
SOTOCOLOR COLORS
DAVE SHARPE LETTERS
MIKE HORWITZ ASSISTANT EDITS
NATE COSBY EDITOR
JOE QUESADA EDITOR-IN-CHIEF
DAN BUCKLEY PUBLISHER
ALAN FINE EXECUTIVE PRODUCER
THE END

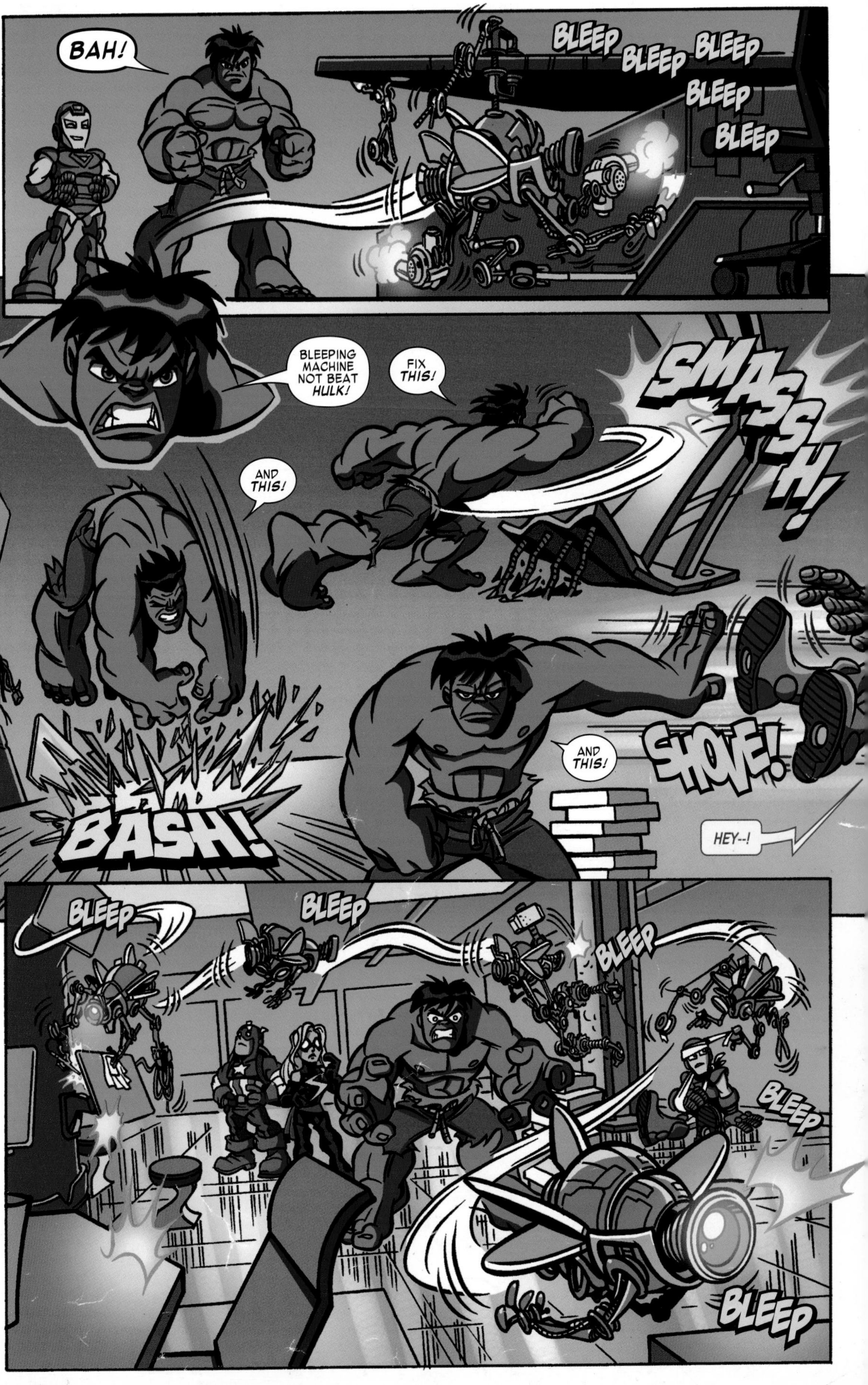
BAH!
BLEEP
BLEEP
BLEEP
BLEEP
BLEEP
BLEEPING MACHINE NOT BEAT HULK!
FIX THIS!
SMASSH!
AND THIS!
BASH!
AND THIS!
SHOVE!
HEY--!
BLEEP
BLEEP
BLEEP
BLEEP
BLEEP

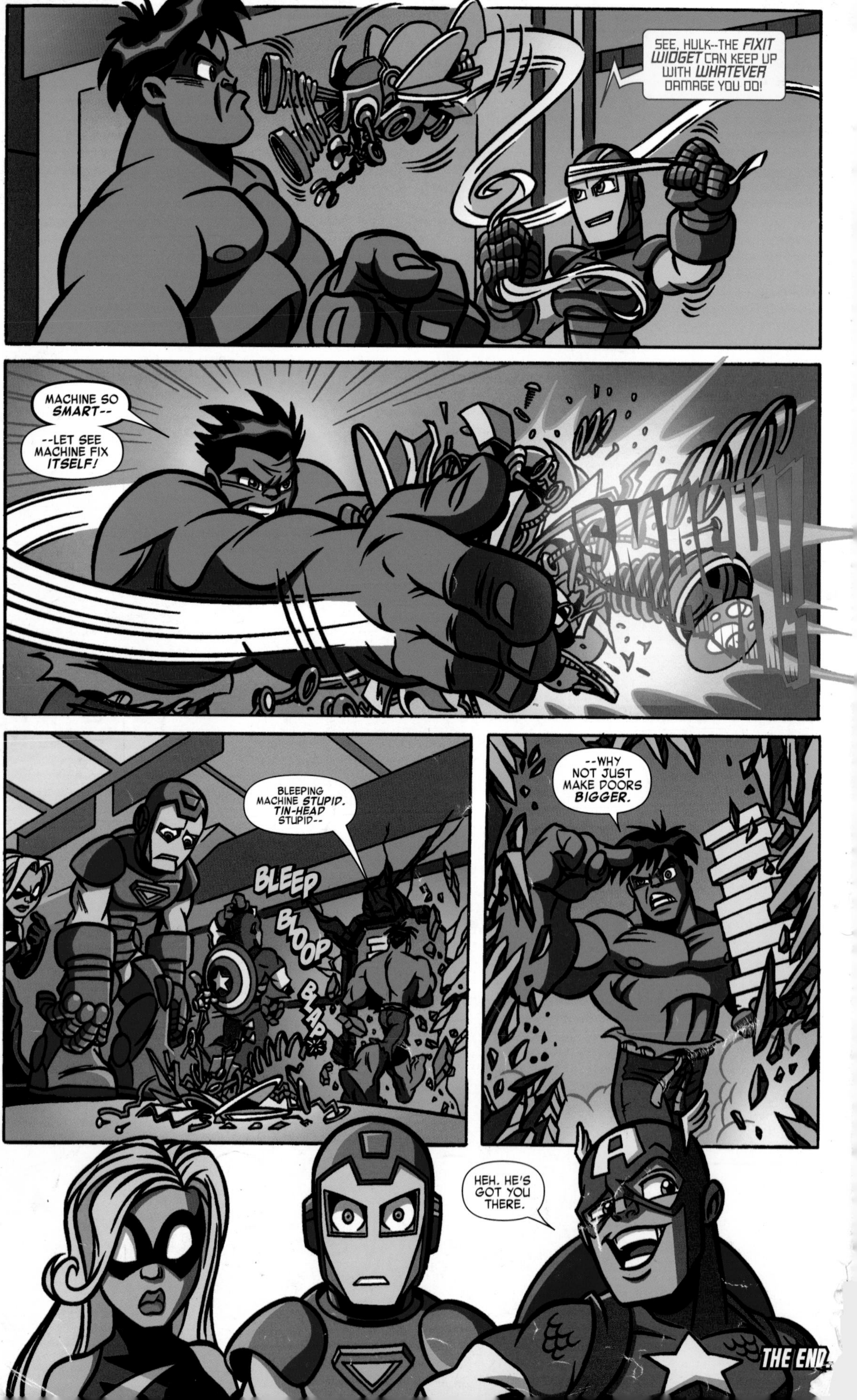
SEE, HULK--THE FIXIT WIDGET CAN KEEP UP WITH WHATEVER DAMAGE YOU DO!
MACHINE SO SMART--
--LET SEE MACHINE FIX ITSELF!
SMASH!
BLEEPING MACHINE STUPID. TIN-HEAD STUPID--
BLEEP
BLOOP
BLAP
--WHY NOT JUST MAKE DOORS BIGGER.
HEH. HE'S GOT YOU THERE.
THE END.

BACK OFF BUB!

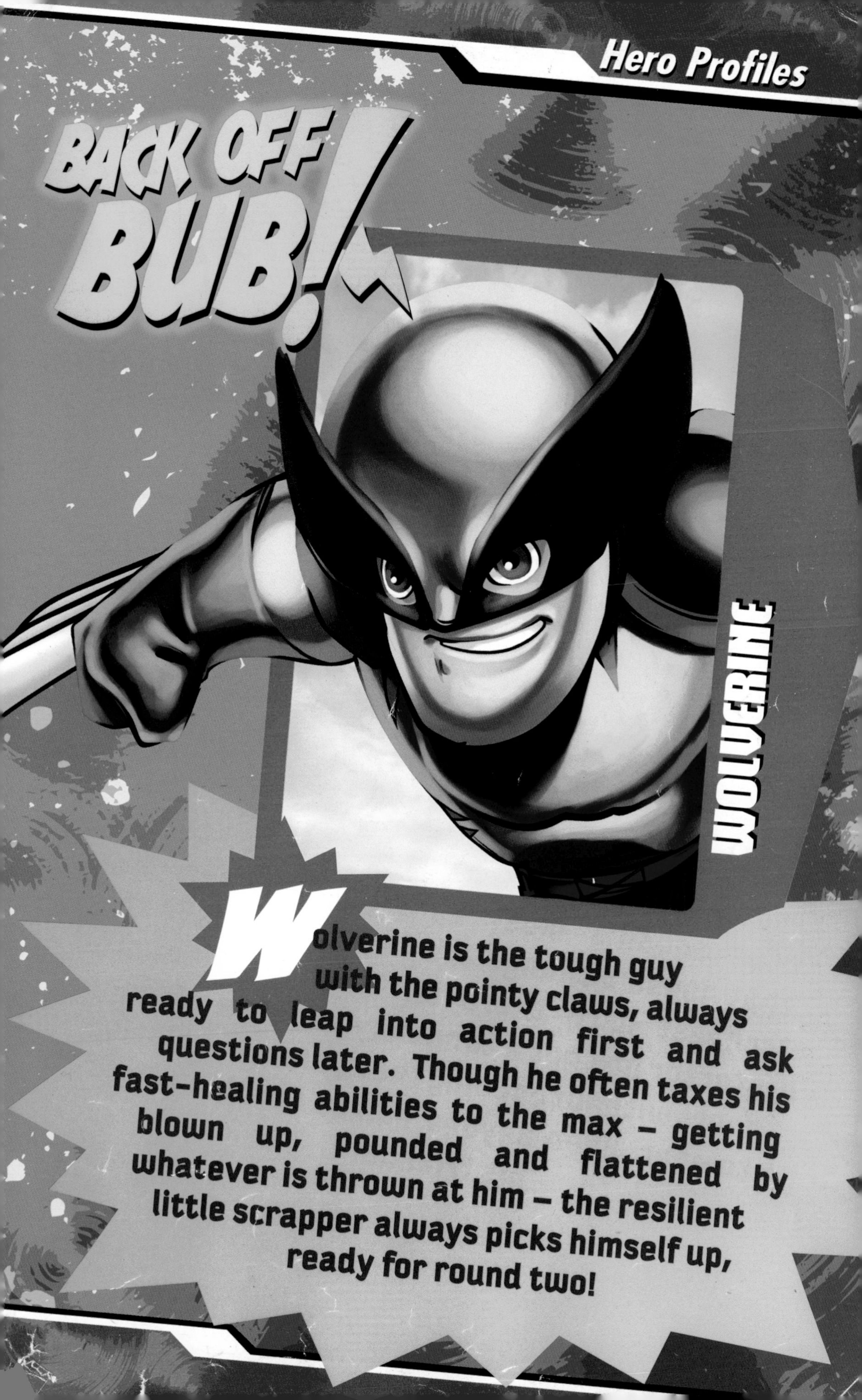
WOLVERINE

Wolverine is the tough guy with the pointy claws, always ready to leap into action first and ask questions later. Though he often taxes his fast-healing abilities to the max – getting blown up, pounded and flattened by whatever is thrown at him – the resilient little scrapper always picks himself up, ready for round two!

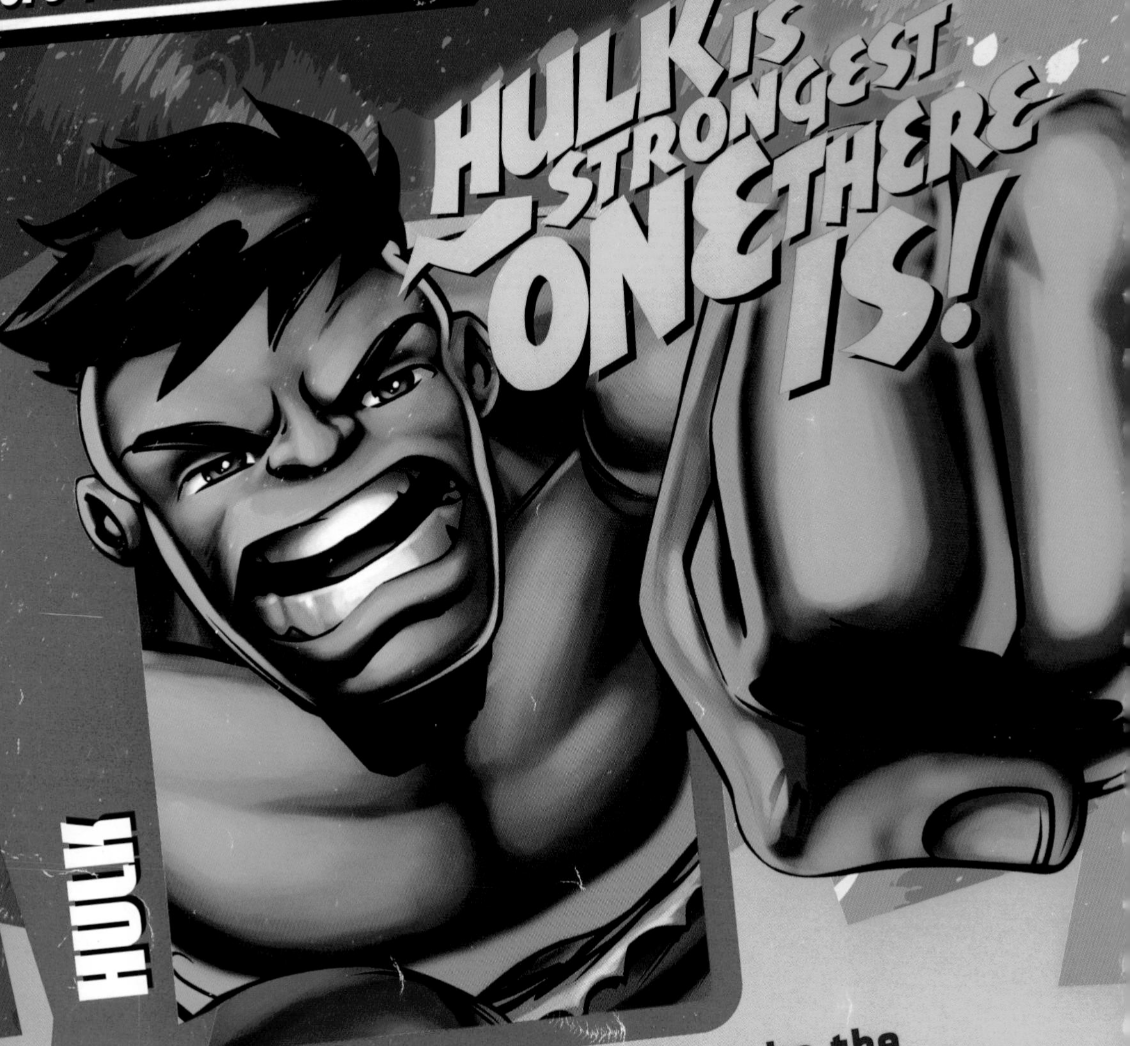
HULK IS STRONGEST ONE THERE IS!
HULK

The big green gamma guy may be the Squad's most childlike member, but that doesn't change the fact that Hulk is the strongest hero there is! This purple-panted protector has got a tendency to crash through doors without opening them, and an explosive temper when anyone makes trouble for his friends!